Operation Busted Flush

Authentic Stories of the Transgender Community Series

Helen Dale

ISBN 978-1999632953

Faced with attacks on their community by the White House Administration, a group of transgender veterans decide to take action

Operation Busted Flush is a work of fiction and any similarity to actual people or organisations, other than as part of the historical background, is purely coincidental.

Surely no one could possibly act in the way that the administration does in this novel.

Could it?

And, even if it did, this novel is not intended to suggest that trans people would react as my characters do; or that such action could possibly be justified.

Operational Maps

South Africa

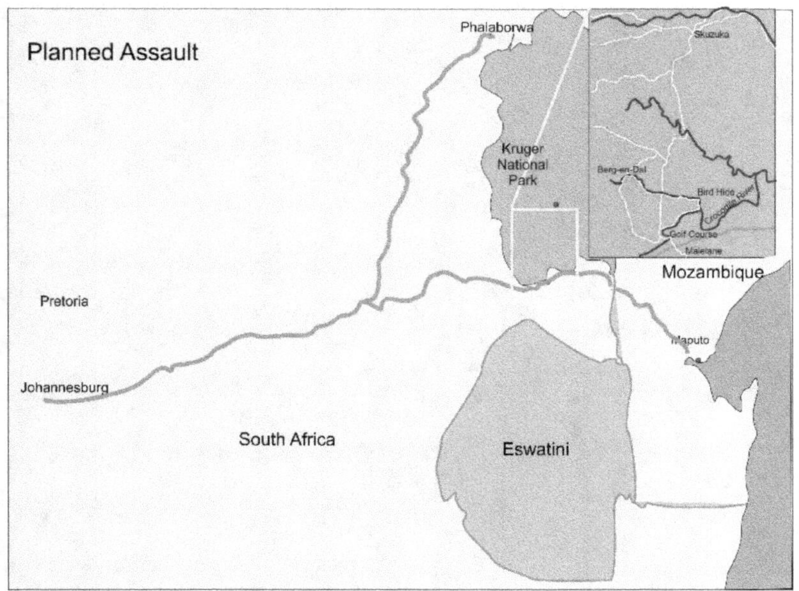

Bali

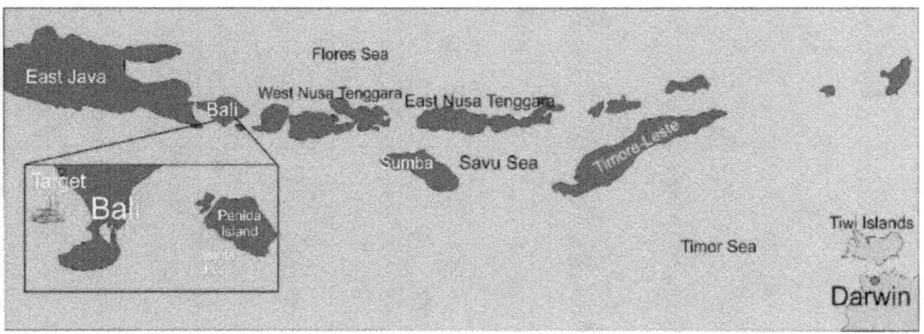

Chapter 1 Situation

Monday 22nd October 2018

And I say the time for waiting is over. He's tried to stop us serving in the military. He's tried to withdraw rights we've fought for. He wants to prevent us using appropriate washrooms. Now he wants to eliminate us completely – they've even taken down every reference to transgender off government websites for Christ's sake! Enough is enough. We have to fucking do something!" Angela slapped her hand on the table.

"You're right — it's time for action. No more pussyfooting around. Let the talkers keep trying to influence opinions — but we need direct action now," agreed Teresa.

"Count me in too," added Rita. "I took an oath to protect the Constitution against ALL enemies, foreign and domestic. He's claimed his orders take precedence over the constitution - so he's declared himself as an enemy."

"Shit, yes," confirmed Teresa. "That bastard has no concept of honour. We all served our country and were prepared to lay down our lives. What has he ever done? Fuck all; other than spend the money his daddy left him and what he could raise with promises of favours. And left a trail of bankrupt companies in his wake."

"Crazy thing is, the British are about to announce that women, including transwomen, will be eligible for front-line service, including in the Regiment." Jacqui didn't need to clarify which 'Regiment', there was only one worth mentioning in this company, 22nd Special Air Service. "I'm in."

The rest of the group all signified their agreement.

"Don't forget the guys too," reminded Rita. "They'll want to be involved, I'm sure. And Pat. This is going to affect NBs as much as the rest of us — if the proposal is to only have male and female — where would that leave non-binary folks?"

"OK — but let's keep the planning group manageable and secure. Rita: you know Jonathan well, don't you? See if you can get him to bring one or two others. I suggest we get together at the weekend. Any chance of using your cabin at the lake, Teresa?" asked Angela.

"Sure. Plenty of room at the shack. Some will have to share but I'm sure we'll cope somehow. Shit we've all put up with far worse conditions in the field, haven't we? I'll get in some supplies, everyone OK with chillies and barbecues? But each person needs to bring their own booze I can't afford the amount this crowd can drink! Or do you see this as a dry weekend Angela?" asked Teresa.

In reality, Teresa was more than capable of paying for everyone's drinks and had done so many times before, thanks to a very successful surveillance business she'd established since leaving the Rangers.

"A few beers won't be a problem — but we'll be too busy working out a plan for really serious drinking," answered Angela.

Angela had naturally taken the lead. She'd been a Major in Delta Force and was now President of Pacific Coast Trans Network. Almost all of the others had seen service with US forces in Iraq or Afghanistan or both or in close protection before transitioning.

Jacqui was one of the exceptions. At 64 she was the oldest — and the most experienced — of all of them. Originally English, she'd moved to the USA in 2012 to join her daughter, son-in-law and granddaughter.

She'd grown up on a rough estate in South Manchester and joined the British Army as soon as she could and completed selection for the SAS at her first attempt when she was 21. She'd seen service in the Falklands, Northern Ireland, the Gulf War — working behind Iraqi lines searching for Scud missile launchers; then in Sierra Leone and Afghanistan and in Iraq again for the war to depose Saddam Hussein. She'd completed her service as a Squadron Sergeant Major, having repeatedly declined to apply for a commission. As SSM, she could stay with the regiment permanently; as an officer (or Rupert) she'd have been limited to two-year tours. Of course, if anyone had realised that Jacqui was trans during her service she'd have been instantly dismissed.

It was only when she retired after thirty years service followed almost immediately by her wife contracting cancer and dying just four months later, that the drive she'd suppressed for decades emerged and she started to transition.

As she drove home from the group that evening, Jacqui thought about her granddaughter. Charlotte, who was now fifteen, had been christened Charles but, when they heard about Jacqui's transition, announced "That's how I feel too." Being able to help support Charlotte had been the deciding factor that had taken Jacqui to the US.

Charlotte's parents, Heather and Barry, had been cautious but sought advice and hadn't tried to suppress what their child was telling them. They'd agreed to her being prescribed puberty blockers and, after a period of limiting dressing to outside school, had seen the headmistress and told her about Charlotte. The school had been equally cautious but supportive. There'd been inevitable problems with some bigoted parents and a handful of the school staff but the head had been adamant and made it clear that they would respect Charlotte's decision and if any staff didn't like it, they could leave. Similarly, any parents who were unhappy with the school's ruling were at liberty to go elsewhere. Few did.

Tuesday 23rd October 2018

Inevitably, the dinner conversation concerned the leaked memo from the White House about the proposal to permanently identify individuals by their genitalia at birth and not allow changes to legal gender.

"I can't let them force me to stay male. They have no idea what being trans feels like. I just can't do it. They have to see that I'm really female and let me live as one," Charlotte cried.

"Don't worry darling, we won't let them do that to you," her mother promised — though how they'd keep that promise, she had no idea. She just knew that she would have to do whatever she could to ensure that her daughter didn't become just another of the dreadful suicide statistics.

"California needs to cede from the Union if that passes," said Barry.

"Maybe we'll have to move to Canada or back to the UK," suggested Heather. "Sorry Barry, but I'm not going to stay in a country that doesn't recognise Charlotte."

"I'm 100% with you, honey, I don't know what my country is becoming under this administration," assured her husband.

"Let's hope that won't be necessary," said Jacqui. "A group of us from PCTN are meeting this weekend to see what we can do. I'll be away from Friday. Don't worry Charlotte, we're determined to prevent this latest insanity from affecting you or anyone else like us." She saw Barry's intense look from under hooded eyelids and held his stare for a few moments before Barry shook his head and reached for his coffee cup.

Friday 26th October 2018

Friday morning, Jacqui packed her Bergen. The distinctive framed rucksack with its DPM — disruptive pattern material — had served her well through years of service around the world. She didn't need a lot of the kit she would normally have stowed in the various pouches for this trip but it felt right to use it rather than a holdall or suitcase. She then joined the rest of the family for breakfast.

Charlotte and Heather hugged Jacqui as she stood by the front door preparing to go out to Angela's Mercedes GLC now waiting for her at the kerb.

"Just be careful Jacqui," cautioned Barry.

"We're only going to be talking. No need to worry," Jacqui assured him.

He'd raised his eyebrows. "Yeah, sure," he'd said.

Barry picked up Jacqui's Bergen. "Come on, I'll walk to the SUV with you."

At the kerbside, Barry hoisted the bag into the back then Angela closed the liftgate from the driver's seat.

"I'm not a fool you know, Jacqui. I'm aware of your background and Angela's. I may not have spent as long in the military as you two — but I can recognise signs of someone preparing for a mission — and using your Bergen tells me exactly what your mental state is right now. I don't know what you have in mind but I know whatever it is, it's for Charlotte's benefit and all the others like her. So, if there's anything I can do to help, let me know."

"I have no idea what you're talking about," Jacqui replied with a smile. "A gang of us are just going up to Teresa's cabin for a chat and to have a few drinks and a barbecue."

"Fine. Well, I've said what I wanted to say. So, have a good weekend."

"We're picking up Rita and Gina on the way," Angela told Jacqui as they pulled away from the kerb. "Teresa is collecting Isabella and the supplies. Denzel is bringing Jonathan and Joseph. Yvonne is bringing Leah, Camila and Malika in her RV. Pat is coming on their motorbike."

"Sounds perfect. Carrot top may just have bitten off more than he can chew this time."

"Well, let's not underestimate the opposition. It's pretty formidable."

"So are we."

"Too fucking true."

"Rita should be along this block. Twelve thirty-six — ah, here we are Twelve fifty-four. Yep, there she is."

"Lovely morning girls. Perfect for a weekend in the mountains," remarked Rita as she slung her pack into the back of the Mercedes then climbed into the rear seat.

Their next stop was only just over a mile for Gina.

Then it was head east out of the city on I-580 and I-120 past Yosemite to Teresa's cabin. The drive took nearly five hours including a comfort break and lunch at a diner where they took the opportunity to refuel the SUV.

As they reached the cabin, they could see that Yvonne's RV was already parked up next to Teresa's Range Rover, Yvonne was another Brit. She'd been in 14 Company, based in Northern Ireland on undercover operations during the late 1980s.

The earlier arrivals had already unloaded the supplies and stored them in the kitchen. Teresa came out of the front door wearing a barbecuing apron.

"Hi gang, Welcome to the lodge. Angie, you're in the second bedroom on the main level; I'm in the other. Jacqui's in the first room on the left on the upper level; Rita and Leah are sharing the room next to Jacqui, Gina you're at the end of the corridor."

"Sounds perfect. This is some 'shack' you've got here."

"It suits me. Good for entertaining clients, of course, excellent fishing in the lake. There's a hot tub out back if anyone wants to chill out later. What's the order of business for the weekend?"

"I figured we need to agree what we aim to do — work out what intelligence we'll need and how to obtain it; then start to work up mission plans."

"When are the others expected?"

"They should be here anytime in the next hour or so," Teresa told her.

"Fine, well, why don't you get yourself squared away then grab a beer? I'll be in the kitchen preparing a pot of chilli for dinner."

"I'll do that but I want to get set up for the planning meeting later — I assume the television in the main lounge has an HDMI socket I can plug my laptop into?"

"We can do better than the lounge, there's a home movie room. The screen in there is even bigger than the one in the lounge. There's also an interactive whiteboard, flip charts and the like. We use it for corporate strategy meetings. It's next to the den which we use for break-out groups if necessary."

Just then, the growl of 900cc of thoroughbred motorcycle engine announced Pat's arrival on their Triumph Bonneville.

They removed their helmet, and shook their head to allow their long blond hair to fluff out after being confined. "My God that's one hell of a fabulous ride out here on those winding roads up over the hills. Absolutely incredible. The guys should be about half an hour behind me, I passed Jonathan's pickup just before Tenaya Lake."

Angela looked at her watch and nodded her head. "So, about five?"

"About then, if they don't stop on the way."

"Your room is on the upper-level second on the right off the balcony," Teresa told Pat. "There are plenty of beers in the fridge once you're unpacked."

As predicted, Jonathan's pickup arrived a little over half an hour later. The transguys unloaded their kit and put it in their room. Everyone then gathered in the dining room for the meal that Teresa had prepared.

"Needs a bit more chilli," joked Gina as she reached for her beer to quench the fire that had erupted in her mouth.

The twelve-quart pot of chilli and the four quarts of rice were soon emptied. The crockery, cutlery and pots were loaded into two dishwashers and left to clean while the team refilled their coffee mugs or picked up another beer and took them into the theatre.

Chapter 2 Mission

26th October 2018

Angela stepped up to the podium. She glanced around the room at the assembled group — most of whom were ex Special Forces or Close Protection.

"OK. I think we know why we are here. POTUS and his VP have declared war on trans people. Make no mistake, it's going to result in thousands of deaths. Calls to trans help lines have quadrupled since the announcement and suicides are already up. And that's just in the first week. Does anyone see this as any different to the way the Nazis introduced anti-Jewish policies and where that led? No? Then we need to take action now to protect our community. I've asked you here to discuss what that action should be and how it can be implemented."

"As I see it, we have three options," said Teresa. She held up a single finger. "One. Hope for the best, that he's flying a kite and will back down."

She extended a second finger. "Two. Campaign against the changes and hope the mid-term elections make it impossible for him to change the law and that he'll be beaten in 2020."

She looked around the room and extended a third finger. "Three eliminate him now. Even if he can't pass new legislation, he can still issue executive orders which are damaging"

"One problem is that if we did get rid of POTUS, the VP is even more anti LGBT. We could get rid of both of them but are the next few in line any better?" asked Rita.

"Two are retiring this year. There are a couple of front runners for their posts as Speaker of the House of Representatives and President Pro Tempore of the Senate. The Secretary of State is next in line after them," added Isabella.

"We're seriously talking about eliminating the top echelon of government, are we?" asked Jonathan.

"Do you see any other way of stopping the insanity at the White House?" Angela asked.

"To be honest, no. I just wanted to be clear what we are talking about."

"Does anyone really think any other option will work?" probed Leah.

"I wish I could think of something — but I can't. The evangelical right has too firm a hold on the VP," remarked Joseph.

"You can't even debate the issue with any of them. They are using trans as a diversionary target. Most people don't care what happens to us. They may say they support our rights but they aren't going to man the barricades for us, are they?" pointed out Yvonne.

"Sad, but true — as Angela stated, it's just like Germany in the thirties," added Jacqui. "Who was it said 'they came for the Socialists and I didn't speak out' Neimeir or something like that".

"Martin Niemöller," confirmed Yvonne.

"Of course, if the Republicans lose their majority in either the House of Representatives or the Senate, it's almost certain there'd be a Democrat or two in the order of succession," remarked Bella.

"We can certainly hope — but let's initially plan on that not being the case," said Angela.

"You realise if we go ahead with this, even if we survive, they'll throw away the keys," noted Jonathan.

"We've faced similar odds before when following orders that often turned out to have nothing to do with the excuses we were given," said Camila. "We may have sworn an oath to obey the president but that only applies to legal orders as I see it. Defending the constitution comes first and he's claiming his orders take precedence so he's made himself a legitimate target."

"If we do come through, chances are we'll have to leave the country," added Isabella.

"Maybe — but it's possible they won't know we've transitioned. Any records they may have on us are likely to be in our birth gender," Joseph pointed out.

"Frankly, as far as I'm concerned, it doesn't matter. If we make it, great. If we don't then I'd rather buy the farm stopping this megalomaniac than dying of boredom — or cancer," said Pat. "At least this really is worth fighting for."

"Shit, how many times were we sent into action with the clear aim of eliminating someone who was a serious threat to the West? They weren't tried by judge and jury — we accepted that they needed to be taken out with the minimum of fuss and we did it. It was just a case of on target, tap-tap, x-ray down, job done," said Jacqui coldly.

"Is everyone agreed? Is everyone on board? Now's the time to back out if you have any doubts," asked Angela.

A murmur of "Fuck yes," "Shit, I'm in," and "Damn right," circled the room.

"OK. We've all got experience of planning covert operations so does anyone disagree with the Mission Statement being to eliminate the threat to the lives of trans people presented by the current White House administration?" Angela continued.

Nobody disagreed.

"OK. Now if we take out the targets individually, they'll each be replaced and we may not be any better off. And, as soon as we hit one of them, security will be beefed up on all of the others. So, we need to take them all at the same time or, at least, so close together they don't have a chance to react," Angela added.

The others nodded their heads, recognising the truth of Angela's words.

"We'll plan on hitting them once we know who will be third and fourth in the hierarchy. The new Speaker may be an opponent of POTUS and less likely to push an anti-LGBT agenda. It may even be a Democrat if the mid-terms go against POTUS. If so, we may have just the two targets. If others take over, we may need to add them to the list," she continued.

"Maybe we should re-create the Pack of Cards idea used in Iraq for key targets," suggested Jacqui. "POTUS as ACE of Spades, VP as KING, Speaker as QUEEN, President of the Senate as JACK and Secretary of State as the TEN. Gives us a Royal Flush to go for if necessary."

"I like it. We'll refer to the operation as Royal Flush and only discuss the targets by their card names from now on," confirmed Angela.

"OK, we need to look at each individual's schedule from early next year to see what they are likely to be doing. The details will be secret but we should be able to get an idea of the sort of activities they'll be involved in."

"ACE is easy — he'll be at the White House, on official visits or playing golf," said Pat. "KING will be at the Executive Office Building, the White House, on official visits or at church."

"I may be able to help there," said Denzel. "I worked on the White House IT system. I needed to test various aspects so I set up dummy accounts. They had different access levels including one that is top-level administrator. I also set up a back door so I could remotely access the system from home. I kind of forgot to remove them when I left." He glanced round the room with a grin.

"That's brilliant. Right, we won't know who the targets are until January. Let's work on the basis of targeting them over the Easter holidays." Angela stepped over to the flip chart and uncapped a marker pen. "We need to find out: 1. Where each of the cards will be next April 19 to 22; 2. Potential opportunities to hit them; 3. Possible methods; 4. Timings when we can hit them simultaneously or at least close enough to avoid alerting the other cards. Then we can get down to tactical approaches. Agreed?"

There were nods of assent from each of those present.

"Ideally, we should work in cells for security — but we all know each other in any case and I think there'll be more value in being able to draw on each other's experience. Does anyone disagree?"

No-one did. So, Angela continued:

"Pat, you were in the Secret Service, can you head up a group to establish where ACE and KING will be and when; and potential opportunities to hit them? Jonathan, you were in Diplomatic Protection – can you do the same for QUEEN, JACK and TEN?" Angela asked.

"Sure," said Pat. "Not going to be too many opportunities that the Secret Service won't have covered in depth; but we'll find something."

"Same with DP," said Jonathan.

Angela looked across the room. "Denzel, I'd like you to focus on getting into the Congress IT and Comms systems."

"Fine Angela. Can I have Isabella to help? She's worked on similar systems."

"You OK with that Isabella?" Angela checked.

"Fine with me," she replied, smiling at Denzel.

"Joseph, can you, Rita, Yvonne and Leah work with Pat? Gina, Malika and Camila with Jonathan. Jacqui, Teresa and I will start to look at Command and Control and Logistics. We'll also use code names for ourselves in any plans. The different groups will be my team, Mako; Pat's will be Bull; Jonathan's Tiger and Denzel's Leopard."

"I like it, "said Rita, "a shiver of sharks — very appropriate."

"Right, let's break into sections and start planning. There are laptops with internet connections through proxy servers for security. Use any of the other rooms on the ground floor."

Later, Angela called for everyone's attention.

"It's now zero dark fifteen – let's hit the sack folks. Breakfast at zero seven thirty, we'll have an update session at zero eight thirty so we all know where we stand. OK?"

27th October 2018

The teams gathered again in the briefing room after breakfast. Angela took the rostrum again. "OK let's hear initial ideas from each section. Pat?"

Pat took Angela's place.

"ACE will be visiting South Africa. His excuse is talks with their President; ostensibly about trade links and defence — but it seems likely that they are just as interested in a joint deal to take over Crocodile River Country Club. ACE will certainly stay at the club and play golf and go on safari while there. The club's about 25 klicks from the Mozambique border and sixty from the coast. The safari might give an alternative opportunity.

KING and his family will be in Zermatt for skiing before he visits some European Heads of State. We have some ideas for taking them out which we'll work up more today. Sundays, he'll be in church."

Jonathan took over from Pat.

"There are two likely republican candidates for QUEEN, which we've designated QUEEN of Spades and QUEEN of Clubs. We're still trying to establish where they'll be. If the Democrats win the House of Representatives, we've designated their candidate QUEEN of Hearts.

"JACK is expected to be sailing his yacht, probably entertaining some guests that he'd much rather the fellow members of his congregation didn't get to hear about. We could just release that information rather than terminate him.

"Our information about 10 is that he is making noises about agreeing with ACE and KING — but doesn't really support them. I'm not suggesting he'd increase our rights but his focus is on other areas. At this stage we don't have any details on where most of these are likely to be in April — in most cases, it depends on the mid-terms and what their roles might be."

"Comments?" invited Angela.

A general discussion with input from all around the room followed for a little over an hour before Angela drew it to a close.

"OK, let's split into our groups again and develop the plans as far as we can taking account of the comments we've just heard. I know there is a limit to firm information about QUEEN, JACK and TEN as that depends on the mid-term election results but you can work out what you don't yet know and need to know and how you can obtain that intelligence. We'll reassemble here at fifteen-thirty. There's bread, cheese and cold meats in the refrigerator and coffee on the hotplate — help yourselves when you want lunch or a drink. Questions? No? OK."

By the afternoon, the planning groups had identified the 'knowns' and the 'known unknowns' and how they would find the answers to the latter; and they'd war-gamed as many scenarios as they could to recognise and minimise the 'unknown unknowns'.

Once again, the whole team reassembled in the cinema to present their ideas to the others.

At the end of the plenary session, Angela announced "OK folks, that will do for today. We'll have another group session in the morning to consolidate the feedback into each group's plan. This evening, we'll relax and have a barbecue and a few beers — I think we've all earned it. I suggest we meet back here again over the weekend of 11th -13th November by which time we'll know the result of the mid-term elections."

Chapter 3 Mid-Term Elections

7th November 2018

Jacqui, Heather and Barry had actively canvassed friends and neighbours to vote democrat — not that there was any realistic chance of the republicans winning their local seats. Charlotte, although too young to vote herself, had been campaigning online pointing out the impact on diversity issues across the board of the administration's instructions.

Charlotte and Jacqui had prepared a meal ready for her parents to get home from work and they ate it while gathered around the television as the first results started to come in from the east coast. The predictions had been for a 'blue wave' sweeping the Democrats to control of both the House of Representatives and the Senate.

"Too close to call at the moment," remarked Barry as the announcer relayed the first few results.

"Certainly not the 'blue wave' we were hoping for," agreed Heather dejectedly.

"Surely the Republicans can't win, can they?" asked Charlotte anxiously.

"Well, darling, the democrats have gained four seats in the House – but the republicans are holding their own in the Senate," Jacqui reassured her as she saw the possibility that if they took out ACE and KING, there would now be a democrat president.

An hour later, the pundits were firmly predicting that the Republicans would retain the Senate but, with 13 seats gained so far, the Democrats were on course to take the House of Representatives.

Then, just before eight, Charlotte let out a shriek.

"Massachusetts has voted to confirm protection for trans people in a referendum. Is that the first time the public has openly voted to support trans, Gran?" she asked as she hugged Jacqui.

"As far as I know, darling. That certainly shows how out of touch the president is. But don't get too excited — as important as it is, that's just in one state. It's not likely to affect the administration's policies"

"I know Gran, but even so, it's brilliant news."

More good news followed as two transgender candidates were elected to state legislatures.

"Ha! Now that's justice," declared Heather. "That clerk who objected to giving marriage licences to same-sex couples has lost her seat."

"Serves her right!" agreed Barry.

"OK, young lady. Most of the seats still to be declared are on the West Coast so it's clear the democrats have now taken control of the House — so off to bed with you. You have school in the morning and it's gone midnight."

"Aw, Mum, can't I stay up a bit longer?"

The look her mum gave her made it clear she would brook no argument so Charlotte kissed her gran and mum and dad and reluctantly climbed the stairs.

"How does this affect your plans, Jacqui?" Barry asked quietly.

"What plans?"

"The plans to remove the President and VP."

"I don't know what you mean. That sounds like something that could be illegal; so, if I was involved in anything of the kind, talking to you about it would amount to conspiracy. Now, you couldn't afford to be involved in anything like that — so I couldn't discuss it with you, could I? In any case, it's all irrelevant as there are no plans."

Barry shook his head and smiled.

"OK, Jacqui. I hear you. But if you need anything for one of your fishing trips up to the lake just let me know."

"Barry, your responsibility is to look after my daughter and granddaughter. Do that and I'll be happy. We can take care of anything else that needs to be done."

Chapter 4 Busted Flush

11th November 2018

The weekend after the elections, the planning group reconvened at Teresa's cabin.

"OK folks, it's virtually certain that QUEEN will be a Democrat. She will be designated QUEEN of Hearts — which now means we have a busted flush, but that's to our advantage in this case as she will be second in the order of succession. The republican candidate is designated QUEEN of Spades. JACK is currently Hatch but he has announced that he will retire on January 3rd. We should have confirmation of both QUEEN and JACK by January 4th. Unless ACE replaces him in the meantime, TEN is unchanged," Angela announced.

"How do you see QUEEN being a democrat affecting our plans?" asked Rita. "Do we now discount JACK and TEN?"

"Not at this stage. I think we should continue to plan to take out JACK and TEN in case we need to. We can always abort those missions if appropriate," replied Angela. "What do others think?"

"I agree. There's always the remote possibility of QUEEN being taken out of the equation at the critical moment and we don't want to see JACK or TEN become POTUS by default," remarked Teresa. "Perhaps we should consider keeping a watch on QUEEN in case someone else sees her as a target if she gets in the way of ACE's ambitions."

"Good point," confirmed Angela. "Team Tiger can you include that in your brief?"

"We could," said Jonathan "but it would stretch us a bit thin on the day."

"Fair comment, OK, we'll set up another team to protect QUEEN; we'll designate it team Nurse. Joseph, your experience in the police would be useful here, can you head this up? We'll need to find someone else to work with you on it does anyone have any ideas?"

"I think so — I was chatting to someone last week at the group. They're ex-diplomatic protection, maybe you know them, Jonathon. Her name is Diane. Last posting was Athens," replied Joseph.

"Tall, short blonde hair, slim?" asked Jonathan.

"That's her."

"Yes, in fact we worked together five years ago in Rome — it was quite a surprise when we recognised each other at the group. Do you want me to approach her or do you want to?"

"Maybe we can do it together?"

"Good idea."

"Right — that's sorted. For this weekend, Jacqui will work with you Joseph. Everyone happy?"

Murmurs of agreement circled the room.

The group broke up and moved to their breakout rooms; most collecting mugs of coffee from the kitchen en route.

Chapter 5 Hammerhead

February 2019

In February, TEN flew down to Antigua in a Cessna Citation jet owned by one of his main supporters. Sipping a twenty-one-year-old Bourbon which had been served by an attractive stewardess, TEN turned to his host.

"That's a hell of a drop of Bourbon — I saw some on sale for around two and a half thousand dollars."

"Only the best for important friends."

TEN took another sip and rolled it around his palate.

"This is damned hospitable of you, Carl; and I want you to know that I really do appreciate your support. Once we get this government shutdown sorted, I'll get that new construction contract sent to you. Those damned Democrats are just being obstructive. We'll build the wall one way or another."

"Well, between you and me, Mr Secretary, I'm not at all convinced that it will actually be effective. There are always ways around, under or over barriers."

"Of course, it won't, but we have to be seen to be honouring the promises that POTUS made to get elected. In the meantime, some of our friends will benefit from the work."

"Indeed; here's to walls then."

Carl placed his empty coffee cup on the table and stood up. "I hope you don't mind me deserting you, Mr Secretary, but I like to keep my hand in flying so I'm going to the cockpit for a while. Pamela here will take care of anything you want. Pamela, anything the Secretary wants, he gets, OK?"

Pamela smiled at TEN, the tip of her tongue licking her upper lip as she did so. "Of course, sir."

TEN looked into her eyes and raised his eyebrows.

As the cabin door closed behind Carl, the other two looked at each other.

"Was there anything I can do for you right now?"

TEN held up his glass. "A refill wouldn't go amiss."

Pamela poured another generous tot into his glass. Her leg pressed against TEN's as she served him. He slipped his hand around her and briefly touched the stocking-clad calf. When she pressed more firmly against his leg, he became bolder and pressed his fingers against her thigh, just above the knee.

She stepped over his legs so she was straddling him, took the glass of bourbon from him and put it to one side. He reached forward and put his hands behind her, slid them up under her mini-skirt and cupped her ass and squeezed.

Pamela leant forward and took hold of his zip and looked into his eyes; she leant even further forward and brushed his lips with hers. Her right hand pulled the zip down then slipped inside his boxers and took hold of his prick. Released from its constriction, it sprang to attention. She looked down and declared: "Very nice, Mr Secretary. I can see you're a big man."

"God, I so want you," he moaned as she stroked his shaft.

She reclined his seat then straddled him again and lowered herself onto him.

Carl returned to the cabin before the aircraft started its final approach into VC Bird Airport on Antigua. "If you'd like Pamela to keep you company later, Mr Secretary, let me know. It goes without saying that any arrangements are completely confidential."

"That's mighty hospitable of you, Carl. I believe I would like to take you up on that offer."

"Consider it done Mr Secretary. We'll have dinner first then meet the ladies afterwards, perhaps find a nightclub for some entertainment."

"That would be most agreeable."

Once Carl, TEN and Pamela had left the aircraft, the pilot entered the cabin and removed two small video cameras that had been positioned to give a clear view of TEN's seat. She put them amongst the charts and reference books in her Nav-bag. Having cleared customs, she took a taxi to her hotel where she was able to view the recordings on her laptop.

She called Jonathan.

"Hi, Babe. I'm safely at the hotel in St Johns. We had an uneventful flight down and everything went as planned. No technical issues at all. The boss is having dinner with a guest this evening. I should be returning as arranged on Wednesday."

"Ok, darling. Have fun down there — but not too much without me. See you in a few days. Love you."

"Love you too, bye."

The conversation was designed to sound innocent. The chances of the call being intercepted were minimal — though, with the Secretary of State present, there was likely to be enhanced coverage of data originating from the area. So, it made sense to be cautious.

Jonathan now knew that Malika had managed to acquire evidence of TEN's 'Mile-high episode' which would be valuable if they needed to apply pressure later. Another member of Team Tiger, Camila, would now plant further cameras in TEN's room for further liaisons between the Secretary and Pamela. Pretending to be a maid, she would access the rooms while TEN and Carl were at dinner and collect the cameras again the following day.

Chapter 6 Tiger

February 2019

While most of Team Tiger was dealing with TEN, Gina was investigating opportunities to deal with President Pro-tem of the Senate, code name JACK.

She saw him leave from a side door to his house and get straight into a car that had pulled up at the kerb moments before. He hadn't bothered with an umbrella for the few steps — despite the rain. It was only because she was keeping a close watch that she noticed the event, anyone else would have missed it.

She followed in the fake taxi she was using and kept watch on the inconspicuous townhouse JACK had entered on leaving the car that had collected him. Gina saw him appear in the window of a room on the second floor before he disappeared from view as he sat down.

The roof sign on the cab contained a directional microphone that Gina aimed at the window of the room where she'd seen JACK and adjusted the settings. The car windscreens were already covered in rain and the inside starting to steam up but she didn't want to draw attention by activating the wipers or demisting.

"Sorry about meeting in a place like this — but we needed somewhere that wasn't linked to any senior members of the party. This is my secretary's home. She and her husband are at the theatre," she heard an unidentified voice declare. "POTUS and the VP are serious threats to the long-term future of the party. They're only interested in the next four, possibly eight, years."

"Maybe so, but the party selected them. We can't just dump them. Those dumbasses who voted for them would have a fit."

"True, but we have to do something and fast. I don't think we can prevent the House from impeaching POTUS in the long term — there's just too much evidence that'll come from Cohen's confessions."

"But if POTUS is impeached, we end up with the VP as President and that's something we really don't want."

Gina sat open-mouthed. It seemed that the GOP were as concerned about ACE and KING as the trans community was.

"We can't allow both of them to be impeached. That would be really embarrassing for the party. We need to ensure the President makes our guest here VP so he can take over when POTUS is impeached. I think a guarantee of a Presidential Pardon for POTUS by our friend here for any alleged offences would work."

At that moment, the curtains were pulled across the window eliminating the vibrations the directional microphone had been picking up.

Jonathan answered his phone as soon as it rang.

"Hi, Tiger," he said as he picked up the call.

"Hi. I wondered if you fancied meeting up for a drink, say the sports bar at ten?"

"Sounds good to me."

"See you there then."

The conversation had been in code. They had actually agreed to meet in fifteen minutes at a coffee shop.

"We have major developments," Gina told Jonathan. She explained what she had overheard.

"How do you think they'll do it?" he asked.

"They won't want to risk a scandal as well as an impeachment, so my guess is something to do with his health. They've probably got something on KING and can force him to step down. The cabal will then persuade the party to accept JACK as his replacement as VP. Then, when POTUS is impeached, he would replace him."

"Sounds plausible. We need to consider how this development impacts on our plans. For that, we need to know exactly when and how they plan to move on ACE and KING." Jonathon remarked thoughtfully. "OK. Assuming they return to the same location for future meetings. We need to bug any rooms they might use."

"It won't be as easy as bugging a hotel room but it shouldn't be too much of a problem, Yvonne has lots of experience from her time with The Det in Northern Ireland. She should be able to help."

Chapter 7 Hand of God

February 2019

Good morning Mr President. Shall we join in a prayer to beseech God's Blessing on our work?"

"I think that would be appropriate. Mr Vice."

The Veep turned to the president's spiritual guide, "Pastor, would you lead us?"

As she put her hands together and bent her head back to look towards the heavens, others in the room bowed their heads. There was a ripple of 'amen' as she concluded her prayer and all but the President and his VP left the room.

POTUS turned to the television, attracted by his own face appearing — then he turned away as he realised the report was of an incident he'd prefer to forget.

"Mr Vice, how do we stop all this fake news about me?"

"Mr President, the fake news is irrelevant. No true American believes it. It's just the bleeding-hearted liberals. Our polls show you are seen as doing God's work bringing this country back to traditional American values. Our supporters know you are cleansing the country and they love you for it. What we need to do is take more steps in that direction and God will ensure your victory in 2020."

"I do wish he'd give us an easier ride though."

"He only sends trials that you can meet and, through which you become stronger. The economy is doing great. Employment is great. You're seen as being firm with America's enemies — and with our allies; insisting that they pay their fair share of NATO."

"That's true," said POTUS.

"We could do more of God's work — and gain more of his support, Sir. We've done a lot to rebalance the protection for people of faith who object to dealing with the Godless as well as remove the misguided rights that your foreign-born predecessor gave them. We need to influence our allies to do the same in their countries. God will love you for that."

The president nodded his head thoughtfully.

Chapter 8 Bull

March 2019

Rita and Pat re-fastened their seat-belts and straightened their seat backs as the aircraft prepared to land at Heathrow airport after the overnight flight from San Francisco. They now faced an eight-hour layover before the next leg from London to Johannesburg. Not that this was anything new to either of them. At least the Boeing 787 was a great deal more comfortable than the back of a C130 Hercules — and the flightpath into Heathrow would be gentle not the steep dive to the ground employed in Afghanistan to avoid being shot down.

About 800 miles southeast of Rita and Pat, Leah and Yvonne were taking their seats for the second leg of their journey to Turin after a ninety-minute stop in Munich. From there, they would rent a car to drive to Zermatt arriving at their hotel about 17.00 hours. It would be dark by then, so they would start their reconnaissance of the area the next day. In the meantime, they could enjoy a leisurely meal.

As Leah signed the tab for the meal and she and Yvonne moved into the bar, Rita and Pat were boarding the aircraft for their eleven-hour flight to South Africa. Once again, their long experience of napping wherever and whenever they could let them block out their surroundings and sleep until they were woken by the stewardesses for breakfast.

At O R Tambo airport, they collected the Nissan SUV they'd hired and drove out of the car park. Their cover was as tourists on safari in the Kruger National Park.

"We should be at Phalaborwa by six," Rita told Pat as they headed for the N1 freeway. "The South African 5th Special Forces Regiment is based there."

"Have you worked with any of them? Anyone likely to recognise you?"

"I did some training with them about eight years ago — but shouldn't think they'd recognise me now," Rita replied with a grin.

"How do they compare?"

"They're good; especially at counter-insurgency. We'd be wise not to under-estimate them."

"Fair enough," Pat replied. "Traffic is light – far less than LA or Frisco. Should be an easy run. Any music on the radio?"

Rita fiddled with the dials and found a station that suited them both. She took out the folder with their itinerary.

"It's about ninety klicks to Letaba tomorrow. I reckon a leisurely breakfast, stock up with supplies at a supermarket then a gentle drive to the rest camp. There seems to be a picnic site just off the road about two-thirds of the way, next to a small lake. It'd be the touristy thing to do to stop there for some lunch."

"That makes sense. You're the navigator."

"Are you OK playing the husband, Pat? I've never really asked how you feel being NB. I know your passport and driving licence still show male because non-binary isn't recognised; whereas I've been able to change mine. That's so unfair."

"It is, but there are plenty of places in the world where having an X or anything indicating I'm other than male or female could prove dangerous so I'm not sure I'd change my documents even if I could. But, yeah, I'm OK with people seeing me as a guy. Most of the time I feel I'm more masculine than feminine in any case. Hell, I just see it as a cover story."

He paused and looked over at Rita before adding "Maybe the question is, are *you* OK playing my wife and sharing a double room? Especially as we're supposed to be on honeymoon."

"It's no problem at all, *darling,* I'm sure we can put on a display of affection when necessary." She looked at him and fluttered her eyelashes. "You're quite an attractive character after all." With that, she rubbed the inside of his thigh for a moment – then gently punched his arm and laughed.

The next morning as they drove into the park, their views to the side of the road were restricted by dense thorn bush, but they still had tantalising glimpses of elephants, antelopes, zebra and giraffes. Various well-thumbed and annotated guides to the animals and birds of the region lay on the dashboard of the SUV. Powerful binoculars, 'scopes and digital SLR cameras with long telephoto and zoom lenses added credence to their cover story.

At Letaba, as they sat outside their lodge overlooking the river, drinking beers, Rita noticed that the impala and nyala had stopped grazing and were jittery.

"I wonder what's spooked them, Pat," she remarked.

"Good question." He picked up the camera and focussed it on the nervous animals.

"Look," Rita exclaimed pointing.

A leopard had sprung from the bush near the river and was charging at the small herd which scattered in its path. The selected target zig-zagged to try to avoid being brought down but the leopard gradually closed on its prey. Both then disappeared into the bush and out of Rita and Pat's view.

"Wow, that was incredible. Did you get any photos, Pat?"

"Sure did. I just kept my finger on the button. Let's see."

Pat replayed the photos on the preview screen. They'd captured four shots as the leopard had chased the impala.

"That's brilliant, well done, Pat. This trip is certainly one of the best I've ever been on. That's two of the big five for us."

Over the next week, they gradually moved south through the Kruger from Letaba to Satara then onto Skuzuka rest camps. Each evening and morning, like typical tourists, they'd check the noticeboards at reception for reported sightings and drive out to see if they'd be fortunate enough to see the reported animals. They took evening game drives to add to their cover — not that they needed any excuse.

As they'd driven along, they'd recorded the entire trip on video as well as taking literally thousands of still photographs. The files had been transferred to a laptop and retained on memory cards.

As they fastened their seat belts in the SUV outside their lodge at Skuzuka rest camp, Rita turned to Pat.

"OK, this is where we get serious. We take a loop off the S114 after 46 klicks; and come back along the north side of the Crocodile River. We should then get a good view of the golf course ACE plans to stay at."

Pat reset the trip odometer then looked through the windscreen. The dazzling azure sky overhead was cloudless, the sun cast jet-black shadows in contrast. The slightest of breezes set leaves in motion but left even the smallest twigs unmoved.

"Roger that, Rita. Gonna be another hot one. Temperature is already 38 degrees outside; what's that in real money?"

"One hundred, Pat!"

"Sheesh and it's only zero-nine-hundred."

Pat reached over and switched on the air conditioning.

"Phew, that's better," they said as the cooling air started to flow.

Rita gave them an amused look.

"You had it soft in the Secret Service, riding around in air-conditioned limos. We had to deal with worse than this in Desert Storm. It could get up into high-forties C; that's a hundred-and-twenty Fahrenheit."

Pat shook their head as they reversed out of their parking bay; drove slowly through the rest camp and left Skuzuka for Berg-En-Dal.

As on previous days, they took their time heading south; stopping whenever something took their interest, opening the SUV windscreens to examine whatever it was through their binoculars or take photographs and record sightings in their notebooks.

"OK, Pat, here's the bridge — take the left turn ahead. The bird hide is about 12 klicks east."

Visiting the hide gave them the excuse, in the remote case that they had to explain themselves, for returning past the target for their reconnaissance.

By sixteen hundred hours, they were slowly driving along the S114. The Crocodile River lay to their left and the junction to the Timferneni loop was coming up on their right.

"OK, Pat, the next six Ks or so are critical."

Rita opened her door window to give clear shots with the camera; letting the hot outside air flood into the vehicle. Pat stopped the SUV as though they were watching an eagle circling above the river.

"Not a lot of cover this side of the river and the trees on the other side will make direct shots almost impossible when Ace is on the golf course," said Pat.

"I agree. And, if he does go on a safari, we wouldn't have any idea exactly where they'd take him. Let's try further along," Rita replied.

Pat slipped the vehicle back into drive and, after a couple of hundred metres, they turned left onto the Malelane-Skukuza road. They reached the bridge over the Crocodile River and stopped.

"OK, so a clear rifle shot doesn't look feasible. But I do have another thought. Turn around then take the road to Berg-en-Dal," Rita told Pat.

Pat did as they were told.

"So, what's this idea of yours?"

Rita explained.

That evening, in their lodge close to the boundary fence of the rest camp, they examined the map of the area, compared it with the photographs they'd taken and discussed how they could implement Rita's plan.

Satisfied they'd achieved as much as they could, they walked along the path just inside the perimeter fence to the restaurant where they were given a table overlooking the Matjulu dam. Although night had fallen quickly while they'd been planning, a huge full moon provided almost as much light as day and they could easily see kudu and impala, white rhino and other animals drinking at the lake.

"This is just magical," said Rita.

"Certainly is, I'd love to come back again sometime without having to focus on our project."

"Not likely is it, if the plan goes ahead?"

"Might be a bit risky, that's for sure. But you never know."

As they left the restaurant, Pat slipped their arm around Rita's waist; she responded sliding her hand into the back pocket of their jeans and they strolled along the path. They'd played the honeymooning couple several times before but Rita sensed that Pat was holding her tighter than usual.

They passed another couple taking the night air and briefly exchanged pleasantries before the other couple continued on their way. Rita and Pat were facing the perimeter fence, looking down onto the shimmering water of the lake.

Rita rested her head on Pat's shoulder.

Pat looked down at her and she tilted her head and looked into their eyes slightly separating her lips as she did so; her fingers caressed his bum. Pat turned to her and slowly dropped their lips onto hers. She wrapped her arms around their neck and sighed as they kissed.

"Come on," Pat said, "Let's get back to the bungalow."

The next morning, as they were driving towards the park gate, they came across two other vehicles that had stopped on the road.

"Wonder what it is?" said Rita, then, looking in the direction the other spectators were staring, she saw the cause of the interest.

"Look, on the branch of that tree there, it's a leopard. Its head is hidden but you can make out its body and its legs and tail hanging down." She took out her camera and took several shots. They sat and watched for several minutes but the big cat wasn't prepared to put on a display so they decided to drive on.

Out of the park, they took the road to the border to investigate ex-filtration routes to the coast at Maputo. After three days they returned then explored an alternative route through Eswatini to Richards Bay where they'd booked scuba diving trips.

Chapter 9 Briefing

April 2019

Snow had left a thick carpet on the ground and continued to fall as the team reconvened at Teresa's lodge. A roaring log fire in the main lounge welcomed them as they dashed from the vehicles into the warmth of the lodge with their kit.

After an early dinner, they gathered in the home theatre.

Angela looked around from the lectern. Did the team in the White House have any idea what they'd taken on by attacking the trans community? Perhaps they thought they were a load of timid cissies? That they'd lay down and let the GOP walk all over them. Not judging by the group in front of her. These individuals had demonstrated their bravery time and time again and had the medals to prove it.

She tapped on the lectern.

"OK, folks, let's get started. Team Bull, can we have your report first?"

Rita walked to the podium.

"We split Team Bull into two; Bull, comprising Pat and myself, considered ACE and Thresher with Yvonne and Leah looked at KING.

"Pat and I spent two weeks around the Kruger acting as tourists to establish our cover — not that we anticipated any problems. We then spent the last two days across the Crocodile River from the Country Club and Golf Course where we expect ACE to be staying.

"As you can see from the Google Earth image on screen, the club is just north of Malalene in a loop of the river. The land across the river from the golf course is relatively flat and has thick bush providing good cover for a sniper with a range of between five hundred and a thousand metres. Unfortunately, between the river and the golf course is a belt of trees that will prevent any clear line of fire.

"Further to the west, the land starts to rise into the Malalene foothills. The outcrops are beyond the range of a sniper and, in any event, we'd still have the barrier of trees to deal with. So, we propose using a remotely controlled drone."

Rita moved to a table at the front of the room, uncovered a drone and held it aloft.

"We've experimented with a model that provides a video link to the controller, has a payload of nearly three kilos and can be operated from a range of up to eight kilometres.

"Part of the payload will be additional batteries to increase the duration to well over an hour. The remainder will be a C4 explosive with ball bearings packed into one face — effectively like a Claymore mine. We'll fly it to within a few feet of ACE then detonate it."

"If you're flying the drone from outside the range of snipers, won't it be visible for several minutes giving ACE time to take cover?" asked Jonathan.

"In fact, it'll be in plain view for several minutes. Have a look at this."

Rita ran a video. It showed Pat preparing a drone in scrubland; a dummy was standing two hundred yards away. As Pat strapped on the controller and lifted the drone off the ground, the camera panned to a bird of prey circling overhead. It stooped towards the ground near the dummy. An instant before it struck, it exploded; shredding the dummy.

There was a stunned silence before Joseph exclaimed "Shit, I thought the shot of the bird was just filler while Pat got the drone in the air. It looked so natural."

"We'll have it in the air, hovering just to the north of the river well before ACE and his party go onto the golf course," said Pat. "The bird is dropped from the drone once the target is seen going onto the golf course. It acts as a glider circling overhead. Judging from other raptors we saw in the area, there are thermals which will keep it aloft for long enough before it dives."

"Won't there be any sound from the drone?" asked Yvonne.

"It's barely noticeable and as soon as it drops the bird, we fly it up and out of range. The protection teams may well see the bird circling but not the drone itself," replied Rita.

"What's the killing circle for the Claymore?" asked Diane.

"We're aiming for a three-foot diameter. We've watched recordings of ACE playing golf and when he's teeing off or on the green, other members of the party are usually outside that zone. Certainly, the protection team tend to give him plenty of privacy," said Pat. "It's possible that some former colleagues of mine will be part of the detail and I'd prefer not to kill or injure them if we can avoid it."

"How do you propose to get the kit into the reserve? Aren't vehicles inspected at the gates?" asked Yvonne.

"They may be; so, Team One, comprising Rita and myself, will enter the park at Malalene Gate and drive back along a track not far from the fence. Team Two, comprising Denzel, Teresa and Isabella, will then fly the drone over the fence to Team One," Pat explained. "Rita and I will then conceal the kit; then proceed to Berg-en-Dal where we'll will join a Wilderness Trail Safari."

"Team Two will then also enter via Malalene Gate and proceed to Skukuza Rest Camp and register. They will join organised trips that evening and the next day. On the third day, when we have confirmation that ACE is at the country club, they will drive south again. Denzel will drop Isabella and Teresa about 8 klicks from the LUP and they'll make their way across country to where we've concealed the equipment. They'll remain overnight ready to attack the next morning. Isabella will operate the drone while Teresa handles the bird."

Rita paused to take a sip of water.

"Pat and I will be in the reception area at Berg-en-Dal. When the bird strikes, we'll leave the camp and drive to the RV, pick up Isabella and Teresa, who will have cut across country, then head for Skuzuka. We RV with Denzel and Isabella and Teresa transfer across to their vehicle."

"If we're questioned, Pat and I and Denzel will have been seen at the time of the attack. There'll be no reason to connect us with the strike. Our on-going itineraries would include bookings over the next few days at other rest camps. Any questions?"

"How do you see ACE's and the local security forces reacting?" asked Jacqui.

"The biggest threat is the 5th Special Forces at Phalaborwa; that's 250 kilometres away – say four to five hours by road. They could, however, enplane at Hoedspruit and be in the area within two hours. Hopefully, they'll be confused and won't know where the attack came from. By staying in plain view and with alibis for the time of the attack, we should be able to get away with it."

After a few more questions, the group was satisfied with Team Bull's plan and, after a short break, they moved on to Team Thresher's proposal for dealing with KING.

"We're more fortunate in that there is more cover for a sniper and a clearer field of fire to KING's favourite ski run," announced Yvonne as she started to outline their plans.

After a comfort break, Angela turned to the next team leader.

"Jonathon, can we have Team Tiger's report?"

"Our target is, as you know, JACK. We've discovered that he's part of a conspiracy to remove ACE and KING as a significant part of the GOP sees them as a threat to the long-term future of the Republican Party. That suits us, up to a point. Their intention is for JACK to replace KING then, if ACE is impeached, he'd become POTUS," Jonathon explained.

"That's all very well; and I concede that JACK would be less of a threat to the trans community than ACE and KING – but how likely is it that ACE will be impeached," asked Jacqui.

"It's by no means certain — but even if he isn't, replacing KING with JACK would remove much of the evangelical movement's influence over ACE and that would be a huge improvement," responded Jonathon.

"Fair point," conceded Jacqui. "But is it likely that ACE will appoint JACK as VP if KING is removed?"

"The GOP seems to think the offer of a pardon, if it becomes necessary, will be enough. Our proposal, in any case, is to put plans for Jack on ice for the time being and see how the conspiracy develops — I think all of us would be happy to avoid wet work if we can," concluded Jonathon.

"If it does become necessary, the plan would be to take him out while he's on his boat." He then outlined the details.

"Team Hammerhead. Malika?" invited Angela.

"We've acquired compromising videos of Ten during his Christmas holiday in Antigua and on the flight down there. A significant part of his funding comes from a Christian Family Standards foundation that would be far from impressed with his antics. We're confident that threatening to release copies will ensure his resignation."

Angela returned to the podium.

"My view is that these plans are, as I'd expect given our experience, first rate. We started this project reluctantly because we saw no other way of protecting our community. IF, and it's a big IF, the GOP replace Ace and King with more moderate POTUS and VP, then our aims will be achieved without direct action. I propose, therefore, that we defer implementation and keep a watching brief. We can constantly update our plans in case we need to reactivate them. Comments?"

There was a general murmur of agreement.

"I don't know whether to be relieved or disappointed," said Jacqui.

Chapter 10 Conspirators

June 2019

Mr President, I think you need to listen to this recording."

Ace turned to his Senior Advisor. "What is it?"

The advisor pressed play on the digital recorder he was holding.

'POTUS and the VP are serious threats to the long-term future of the party. They're only interested in the next four, possibly eight, years.'

'Maybe so, but the party selected them. We can't just dump them. Those dumbasses who voted for them would have a fit.'

As the recording played and Jack's treachery became apparent, Ace's face turned redder; the pencil he'd been holding suddenly snapped in his fingers and he threw it across the room. Ace turned to his Senior Advisor. "What is it?"

The advisor pressed play on the digital recorder he was holding.

'POTUS and the VP are serious threats to the long-term future of the party. They're only interested in the next four, possibly eight, years.'

'Maybe so, but the party selected them. We can't just dump them. Those dumbasses who voted for them would have a fit.'

As the recording played and Jack's treachery became apparent, Ace's face turned redder; the pencil he'd been holding suddenly snapped in his fingers and he threw it across the room.

"Is that who I think it is?"

"I'm sorry to say it is Mr President."

"How dare he? It's because of me that he's where he is. If it hadn't been for my successes, the party wouldn't have a majority in the Senate. The damned traitor. Get the Vice President in here right now. Get my other advisors here too."

Minions rushed to do as they were bid.

"Where did this tape come from? Are we sure it's genuine?" asked King. "Could it have been faked?"

"It arrived yesterday but we have no idea who sent it. It seems to be recordings of two meetings. The first involves the President Pro-Tem of the Senate and Edwin Millhouse from the national committee. The second also includes the Secretary of State," the Advisor confirmed.

"We have to get rid of them. How do we do it?"

"You can replace the Secretary of State but not the others. The party can fire Millhouse but only the Senate itself can replace its President Pro-Tem," the Advisor paused, reluctant to continue, "But I don't think they would."

"You don't think the party will fire Millhouse — or you don't think the Senate will replace the President Pro-Tem?" demanded the Vice President.

"Both," said the Advisor. "In any case, we daren't make the news public. The liberal media will have a field day with any hint of dissent in the party. We have to show a united front."

"OK, so I'll take care of the Secretary of State but how do we get rid of the other traitors? If I can't fire them and I can't have them arrested for sedition? I suppose it's too much to hope for them to resign or fall ill or something."

Two of the Senior Advisors exchanged glances.

"We'll have words with them. If they know we're aware of their plans, maybe they'll back off. Leave it with us. We'll take care of the problem. Can I suggest you wait until we've spoken to them before firing the Secretary of State? Maybe we can persuade him to resign on grounds of ill health or something."

Chapter 11 Regroup

July 2019

Ok, folks, as you know, JACK was killed last week in an apparent 'hit and run'. Well, that's the story the administration is putting out. Our information is rather different. It seems ACE's Advisors called in a favour from an Eastern European country. It seems we weren't the only ones monitoring the meetings the GOP were having. As TEN has also resigned, we're back to the drawing board as far as those positions are concerned. It will take some weeks before we know who the new incumbents are," Angela announced to the assembled group.

"How does that impact on plans for ACE and KING?" asked Camila.

"That's what we're here to discuss. Obviously, they'll be delayed but we know ACE plans to go back to Crocodile River Country Club later in the year. We'll re-work plans for KING once we have dates. It's not what we originally planned to do this weekend, as you know it was intended to be a final check on preparations. We'll spend this evening considering the implications of the delays and changed targets – then just relax for the rest of the weekend. We can probably all do with a break."

"There's plenty to do — feel free to use any of the equipment down by the lake. There are canoes, sailing boats, fishing — or you can use the jacuzzi here at the lodge. Or there are stables just a mile away if you fancy some riding," Teresa told them.

Pat turned to Rita who was sitting next to them. "Ready?" they asked.

"Absolutely," she replied. She and Pat stood up.

"Can I have everyone's attention for a minute?" Rita asked. "As you know, the plan called for Pat and me to play the role of a married couple — well, we won't be pretending. I've asked Pat to marry me and they've agreed to be my spouse. We're getting married next month and we'd love you all to be our guests."

The other members of the group gathered around to congratulate them.

"About time you made it official," said Yvonne. "We've all been wondering how long it would take."

"I hesitated because of the difference in our ages but we eventually decided 'sod it, they're just numbers'," said Rita.

"So, are you going to wear an engagement ring and is it going to be a white wedding?" asked Leah.

"I know it's cis-normative, but yes I am. Pat may be non-binary but I definitely identify as female and I want the full deal," Rita told her. "My parents have been supportive of my transition and they'd have been disappointed if I hadn't gone for a traditional wedding."

"Can I be a bridesmaid?" asked Malika.

"Me too," Leah and Camila clamoured.

"Of course you can, I was going to ask you in any case," Rita replied.

"Have you chosen your dress yet? What's it like?" Camila asked. "Do you have any ideas for the bridesmaids' dresses?"

"I've got some pictures — I'll show you all later."

"What about you Pat? What will you be wearing?" Jonathan wanted to know.

"I thought of going for a gender queer look – mixing a skirt with a masculine jacket but I thought it would detract from Rita's dress and I didn't want to do that. I've settled on a white Tuxedo, very dark plum pants, frilled light lilac shirt with a cravat. I think that says 'mainly masculine but with a strong feminine side' which fits me to a T."

Angela looked at her watch and walked over to have a word with Teresa and Jacqui before saying "OK, there's no urgency to discuss plans this evening — so let's have a bit of a party to celebrate Rita and Pat's news. We'll leave the work sessions until the morning."

"I'll get some champagne from the cellar," Teresa added.

Chapter 12 Re-plan 2

October 2019

Six weeks after Rita and Pat's wedding, the group reconvened at the lodge. Since the previous planning session, the administration had tried to make life even harder for the gay and trans communities.

"Jacqui and I attended the Pacific Coast Queers liaison meeting last month. It seems we aren't the only organisation that is planning direct action against the administration. We were both approached separately about joining one of the groups. We agreed, though, that they are a bunch of amateurs and we should keep well clear of them." Angela told the assembled teams.

"They approached Ange and me because of our experience but they didn't have a clue about what would be involved," Jacqui confirmed.

"We didn't tell them anything about our own intentions, of course," Angela added. "But we'll need to ensure their actions don't interfere with our plans or cause the administration to increase security."

As Angela pulled up at the kerb to drop Jacqui off, they were approached by two men who had stepped out of a Ford Interceptor. Wearing conservatively cut two-piece suits, white shirts with striped ties, dark glasses and with cropped haircuts, they were the epitome of Hollywood plain clothes law officers.

"Uh oh, trouble," Angela murmured.

"Good afternoon ladies, are you Angela Collins and Jacqueline Reynolds?"

"Who's asking?"

"I'm Special Agent Doyle and this is Special Agent Wilson. We're with The Secret Service."

"What's this about? Can we see some identification?" Angela asked.

Doyle glanced at Wilson before taking out his ID and showing it to Angela; Wilson had walked round to Jacqui's side of the SUV and showed her his ID.

"Thank you, gentlemen. Yes, I'm Angela Collins and this is Jacqui Reynolds — how can we help you?"

"We want to ask you some questions about a meeting we believe you attended recently. We need you to accompany us to our office in North Beach. Special Agent Wilson will go with you to ensure you don't get lost."

At that point, Heather opened the front door and walked down the path.

"What's going on, Jacqui?"

"Hi darling, these gentlemen from the Secret Service want to ask us about a meeting we attended recently. Nothing to worry about," Jacqui told her.

"Gentlemen, do you mind if my daughter takes my bag inside? Or will you want to search it — feel free if you do." She undid the zip and opened the overnight bag as she asked the question. "It's mainly dirty laundry but if you want to rummage around ....." she left the rest of the sentence unsaid.

"I don't think we need to search your bags we just need to speak to you about the meeting you attended at the LGBT centre on September 28th."

Jacqui shrugged her shoulders. "Fine. It was just routine stuff with various queer groups liaising over plans for the future. Trans Day of Remembrance, Pride events . . ."

Wilson interrupted. "Let's hold the explanations until we get downtown."

"OK — do we need lawyers present?" asked Angela.

"Up to you. Do you think something's going to come up that means you need one?"

"I can't imagine what," Angela replied.

During the drive to San Francisco's waterfront, Jacqui smiled to herself. She knew exactly what the Special Agents were interested in.

No doubt the Special Agents thought they could extract information from the two of them. Fat chance. As part of her SAS selection, she'd been subjected to 'beasting' after the escape and evasion element. Exhausted, cold and hungry, candidates were subjected to aggressive interrogation bordering on physical torture. Angela would have been through something similar as part of her training with Delta Force. They'd been trained to deal with cross-examination.

At the field office, they were led into individual interview rooms.

"You're not American by birth, are you?" Wilson asked Jacqui.

"No, I came over in 2012 to be with my daughter after my wife died."

"So, tell me about this meeting at the LGBT centre on September 28th."

"It was just the usual quarterly liaison meeting between various LGBT+ groups."

"Who was there?"

"Carol from Pacific Sapphics, Paul from West Coast Bears, Henry from the LGBT Centre, Francesca from the Helpline," Jacqui recited the list of a dozen attendees.

"You've only given first names — do you have their surnames?" asked Wilson.

"Sorry, no, we only tend to work with first names."

"How well do you know Chuck Cartwright from the San Jose Gay Bikers?"

"Not particularly well, enough to say hello but our interests don't really cross over." Jacqui had been waiting for his name to come up as he'd made the approach.

"We've heard he was particularly critical of the President."

"Well, that's not hard for anyone who's LGBT. He's attacked our rights consistently. I doubt if anyone at the meeting was a fan of his — or the Vice President."

"Did he suggest taking matters further?"

"Oh hell, we've all said what we'd like to do to that dickhead but that's all it is — just talk."

"So, there were no discussions about how they'd actually carry out an assassination?"

"What? No, of course not. It was just banter, letting off steam."

"And you weren't involved in any discussion to kill the president?"

"Like I said, we all joked about it and maybe one or two let their imagination loose. But no one seriously suggested taking action; at least, not while Angela and I were in the room. Why? Has someone suggested that they are planning to assassinate POTUS?"

Wilson ignored Jacqui's questions.

"But you didn't report Mr Cartwright to the authorities — why not?"

"For what? Saying what he'd like to do to POTUS? It wasn't a serious suggestion — well, I didn't take it as such. If I reported everyone who'd like to get rid of him, I'd be on the phone 24-7."

"So, what time did you leave the meeting?"

"Nine Thirty."

"And did Ms Collins leave with you?"

"Yes, she was giving me a ride."

"Did you discuss the proposal to kill the President on your way home?"

"Like I said, there was no such suggestion; not a serious one in any case. Mind you, I doubt if any of us would shed a tear if someone did get rid of him."

Wilson gathered up the papers in front of him.

"Ok, well, thank you for your time Ms Reynolds. That'll be all for now."

Jacqui picked up her shoulder bag, stood up and left the room. Angela was waiting for her.

In the car, Angela turned to Jacqui. She felt under the dashboard and winked. They'd known there was a chance of being questioned and that the SUV would be bugged during their interviews. The microphone hadn't been particularly carefully hidden — but it might not be the only one. She'd take the vehicle to Teresa's company to have it swept thoroughly.

"What did you make of that?"

"Can you believe someone actually took 'Hos' Cartwright seriously? How could anyone think he'd try to assassinate the president?"

"I can just see his crew riding into action on their Harley's like an old-time posse on the Ponderosa."

"Do you think he might have been genuine? You and I treated it as a joke, well not a joke as such, but wishful thinking — but could he have meant it?"

"Not a chance." Angela paused as though giving it more thought. "No. Not them."

She turned and smiled at Jacqui as they pulled into traffic.

"What are your plans for this week?" she asked

"Charlotte has an endocrinologist appointment on Tuesday. As you know, she started hormone treatment three months ago so they want to do some blood tests and review her progress."

"Brilliant, well, give her my love, Jacqui."

"Will do. What are your plans?"

"Work as usual. I'll probably meet up with Teresa for a drink one evening. Fancy joining us?"

"Sounds good to me."

Chapter 13 Hold Position

October 2019

On Thursday evening, Jacqui and Angela met up at Teresa's home.

As she passed the others bottles of beer, Teresa asked "Do you think they seriously suspect you of being involved in the Gay Biker's plans?"

"No, I'm pretty sure we threw them off the scent. I think our explanation held up during questioning and our conversation in the truck afterwards should have confirmed it," Angela replied.

"I agree. As you know, we'd anticipated being questioned just because we were at the meeting. The way the bikers were talking, there was bound to be a leak," confirmed Jacqui.

"With any luck, they'll see the trans group as a collection of soft females who would dare say boo to a goose," laughed Angela.

"Even so, we need to take extra care. Let's not get overconfident or rash."

"There's not a lot we can do much before next spring anyway — so let's put plans on the back burner for now," suggested Angela.

The others looked at each other and nodded.

"Agreed."

"Now what do you want to do about the bug they planted in your SUV, Angela? I can remove it if you want and sweep the vehicle for any others."

"Sweep it — but leave any you find in place for the time being. Removing them might seem suspicious."

"Okay, the bug they hid under the dash is voice-activated and has a built-in SIM and recorder. They can call it like a mobile phone to download any recordings but all of that limits battery life. Here, plug this MP3 player into your radio — there's an audiobook of the complete works of Jane Austen. The voice activation ignores engine noise and most music but it'll record as long as the book is playing. That'll drain the battery for them."

"Excellent! Hope they enjoy listening to classics. I'm driving down to Santa Barbara tomorrow. Ten hours there and back should keep them entertained."

It was just before midnight when Jacqui paid off the cab and walked up the drive past Heather's Honda Civic, Barry's Mercedes, her own Jaguar XK and Charlotte's Toyota Corolla. She noticed that the lawn needed mowing and resolved to do it the following day. Opening the front door, she was surprised to hear the family in the living room; she'd expected them to have gone to bed before she got home.

As she joined them, she could immediately see that Charlotte had been crying.

"What's happened?" she asked gently; squatting down in front of her granddaughter.

Charlotte flung her arms around Jacqui's neck.

"It's Bobbi. She's dead. She just couldn't take any more," Charlotte sobbed. Bobbi was one of her friends from the Trans Teen Group.

She looked into Jacqui's eyes seeking to understand, "Why are people so cruel? Why can't they just let us be, Gran? We don't ask to be the way we are. It doesn't affect them at all so why do they hate us?"

Jacqui pulled Charlotte to her.

"Some people are just afraid of anything different; of things they don't understand. Some have to blame someone else for their own failings."

"But why take it out on people like Bobbi and me, or you? We don't want to hurt them — why do they want to hurt us? Some of Bobbi's neighbours kept calling her names and painting things on her house. They even threw rocks through the windows. Why? How can they think that's an OK thing to do? It's been getting worse and worse since those men were in the White House."

"I know. I know, darling. The administration attacking us makes some people think it's OK for them to do the same. We have to do all we can to ensure they aren't re-elected next year."

"But how many of us are going to die before then? How many of our rights are they going to take away from us? How can we carry on with this happening?"

Jacqui pulled herself away from Charlotte but still held onto her shoulders. She looked her in the face and firmly but gently said: "Now listen, things look bad at the moment but we can and will get through it. The LGBT communities have made huge gains over the last forty years. At the moment we are losing some ground but we're still a long way ahead of where we were when I was your age. I'd have been kicked out of the army even twenty-five years ago. Now there are military LGBT staff associations."

"I know you're right Gran. But that doesn't help Bobbi or the others that are attacked and killed."

Chapter 14 Covid

13th March 2020

OK folks. I hope you've all had a restful winter. Now's the time for us to start serious preparations. It's taken us a lot longer than we'd hoped but we're all used to operations being delayed," Angela announced as the group assembled once more at Teresa's lodge.

"Is everyone still agreed that we proceed with the project?" she continued. "There is an increasing likelihood of ACE being re-elected. He's benefiting from the previous administration's economic policy and getting the credit."

A general murmur of assent spread around the room.

"OK, then let's review the individual plans. Pat?"

"Thanks, Angela. Team Bull's plans to deal with ACE remain fundamentally unchanged, apart from the timing. We believe he intends to visit Crocodile Country Club again in May. That's when we propose striking. Let me remind you of the details."

Over the course of the day, each group leader outlined their team's proposals.

At the end of the presentations, Camila raised a question.

"Did anything come of the investigation of Hos Cartwright and his bikers?"

"No. They were given a warning not to even joke about plotting to assassinate the president — but the general conclusion was that they weren't a serious threat and didn't justify any more effort. We got the feeling that some of the agents investigating the report weren't entirely unsympathetic. There was also a suggestion that the report of the meeting had been malicious and homophobic," Angela answered.

"Do we have any intelligence about this virus that's causing problems in the Far East? Do you think that will impact on our plans — is ACE likely to change his schedule?" Yvonne asked.

"As far as we know, from monitoring e-mails, ACE isn't taking Covid that seriously and has no intention of cancelling his trip. The latest information is that he just sees it as a Chinese problem," said Denzel. "His attitude seems to be that the authorities will contain it the same as they did with Zika and Ebola."

"OK. It's just that I've heard rumours that travel might be restricted."

"I guess that's always possible especially travellers from the infected area — but if ACE wants to go somewhere, you can bet he'll go; and you know how he likes his golf!"

"Good point, I just thought I'd mention it," said Yvonne.

27th March 2020

A week later, as San Francisco issued its 'Shelter at Home' order, the optimism was shattered. Teams were able to get together to exercise and the team leaders met with Angela, Teresa and Jacqui using the same excuse.

"It doesn't look like ACE or KING will be leaving the country at present so we're having to put the plans on ice again," Pat advised the trio. "Anyone would think someone up there is protecting them!" They pointed skywards. "Maybe there's something in what KING's evangelical friends have been saying about him being the new Messiah!"

"You could be right. Depending how this pandemic goes, it might work for or against him. If his luck holds, he might just come out smelling of roses. If not, maybe he'll be in the brown stuff," Jacqui remarked.

"Either way, all we can do is keep monitoring the situation and be ready to act when the opportunity arises," Angela said. "Denzel and Isabella are continuing to monitor the White House IT systems so we'll get updates on any plans. They've also set up a secure email system for us — but be careful how you use it.

19th May 2020

Angela was drying her hair when her mobile rang. She put down the drier and picked up the phone, glancing at the display to see who was calling.

"Hi, Pat, how's things with you?"

"I'm OK, It's Rita. She hadn't been feeling too good the last couple of days so she went for a Covid test and it's proved positive."

"Shit, that's unfortunate. But she's young and fit so should be OK."

"Yeah, I'm not really too concerned about her — but she was with Yvonne recently so there's a chance that she might have passed it on to her."

"See what you mean, she's a bit older than me so just on the cusp of a vulnerable category. Even so, she's also always been fit so should be able to fight it off if she does have it. There's not a lot we can do except hope they'll both be OK. Give them our love when you speak to them. How does this impact on plans?"

"It doesn't at the moment. We can't do anything other than keep a watch on ACE and KING; the rest of the team can handle that."

"OK — well keep me in touch."

The news, when it came, wasn't what Angela wanted to hear. Rita had developed complications and had been put on a ventilator. Pat had been unable to visit her even when it became apparent that she wouldn't recover.

14th September 2020

With 'Shelter at Home' restrictions eased the teams met again at Teresa's lodge.

Angela took to the podium.

"It's been quite a summer. As you all know, we lost our friend Rita to Covid and our thoughts are with Pat. Let's take a minute to stand in silence to think of her and all the others who have been taken from their loved ones unnecessarily due to the mishandling of the pandemic." Angela bowed her head.

After a minute's silence, she looked around the room noticing a number of the members wiping tears from their eyes. Yvonne had her arm around Pat's shoulder in support. They were all used to losing friends in battle but this was different. And personal.

"It's beginning to look as though ACE's mishandling of the pandemic and the Black Lives Matter protests are impacting on his chances of a second term. If that's the case then we can stand down. But let's not count chickens. The polls were wrong last time. They were also off over the mid-term elections with the predicted blue wave not happening. Make no mistake, if he does get re-elected, chances are that LGBTQ groups will be in for even more problems.

"In the meantime, there is a real risk of reaction to the BLM movement involving our community too especially the black and latinx members. It's already been the worst year ever for murders of trans people so take care out there folks," Angela continued.

"Keep in mind, too, that if he does lose, ACE is unlikely to go quietly. His supporters are already making noises about armed protests. God knows what executive orders he's likely to issue between November and January," added Teresa.

Chapter 15 Elections

4th November 2020

I t's still too close to call at the moment," the announcer on the television said, "far closer than the polls were predicting. It looks as though it's going to come down to Pennsylvania, Nevada, Arizona, Georgia and North Carolina."

Charlotte took her grandmother's arm, draped it around her shoulder then snuggled into her. "He can't win a second term, can he? That would be awful."

Jacqui looked down and her and pulled her tighter still.

"It depends on the postal ballots. Our guy is leading in leading in Nevada and Arizona and that would be enough," she told her granddaughter. She looked at Charlotte; she'd started hormone treatment on her sixteenth birthday and, as puberty blockers had prevented the development of facial hair and other masculine features, she was a typical teenage girl. Jacqui wondered how her own life would have been different if she'd been able to follow the same path. But, then, she wouldn't have had Heather and Charlotte would never have been born.

"At least openly trans folks have been elected to state offices. It was great to see the guy who proposed the toilet bill was defeated by a trans woman," Charlotte said.

"Yes, and there's still a chance the Senate will flip — though it's disappointing that there haven't been more gains. I just don't understand how we've lost seats in the House though," Heather remarked sadly.

"He can't stop the counts though, can he? Or get postal ballots disqualified? Can he?" Charlotte asked.

"I don't think so, darling," her father reassured her. "He doesn't seem to have any actual evidence of fraud so I can't see what his grounds would be."

Chapter 16 Flight

December 2020

H ave you seen the news?" Jacqui asked as Angela answered her call. "Ace has resigned. King is being sworn in as POTUS."

"Shit, so what's Ace going to do now? Has he been arrested?" Angela asked.

"No. He flew to Andrews in Marine One where he made his resignation announcement. He then immediately boarded his private 757. I suspect he's trying to get out before any warrants can be served."

"I see. Look, let me call you back Jacqui, I'm in the supermarket. Give me ten minutes."

Angela loaded her shopping on the belt at the checkout, paid for the purchases then wheeled the trolley to her SUV in the parking lot. After transferring everything into the back and returning the trolley, she got into the vehicle and called Jacqui back.

"Sorry about that, Jacqui. So, does he think King will pardon him for his crimes? Is that the deal do you think?"

"God knows. But can King pardon all of his crimes? Doesn't he have to be convicted first? Didn't I hear that POTUS can only pardon federal offences and some of the charges against Ace are for state offences?"

"Knowing that crowd, I wouldn't be surprised if they have some way around the problems, Jacqui."

"True. Ah well, Ange, at least we're rid of the bastard — hopefully, he's a spent force. Hopefully, too, the GOP won't want to run anyone tainted by association with him. I don't think he did himself any favours with his behaviour after the election."

"Just a pity he's likely to get off lightly after all the damage he's done. At least 46 has said he's reversing all of Ace's instructions regarding the trans community."

"Ace is lucky to have survived this far. We came so close to being able to implement our ideas. But that's the nature of the beast; the unexpected will always screw your plans and you can never anticipate every eventuality — just be ready to improvise when necessary."

"Is there any indication where he's going?"

"Denzel called while you were in the store. He says they've seen emails suggesting he's heading for one of his resorts in Bali."

"That figures. I don't think Indonesia has an extradition treaty with the US."

"Oh, by the way, FLOTUS wasn't on board with Ace."

Chapter 17 Eagle on Par Four

Jan 2021

Yvonne saw Dougie waiting at the barrier as she, Gina and Pat emerged from customs at Darwin airport. She was engulfed in a firm hug by this bear of a man.

"It's good to see you again, mate. How've you been?"

"Fine Dougie, these are Pat and Gina," she added. "This is Dougie. We trained together back in the day."

"Good to meet you folks. Come on, the Ute's in the parking lot."

They went out into the blazing sun, the heat a shock after nearly two days cocooned in air-conditioned aircraft and airports. It wasn't long, however, before they were in Dougie's twin-cab Toyota Hilux.

"So, Yvonne, are you going to tell me what you're really doing over here? I mean, it's great to see you, but you didn't fly to Oz just to visit me. Your shipment arrived, by the way. It's on the boat."

"You mean you don't believe we're just here to do a bit of sailing and scuba diving?"

Dougie turned to look at Yvonne and screwed up his face. "Do you really think I'm as green as I'm cabbage-looking — as my old mum used to say?"

"Are you sure you want to know?" Yvonne asked in reply.

Dougie took his eyes off the road for a few seconds to give Yvonne a stare.

"There's only one thing that's changed in this neck of the woods recently and that's the arrival of a certain individual. So, I'm guessing that's your reason for coming here and I don't suppose for one moment it's to just say 'hello' is it?"

Yvonne remained silent so Dougie continued: "Now I don't pretend to understand what it means to be trans but I do know he made life difficult for your lot and tried to kick you out of the military. I can't see you taking that lying down."

"You always were too clever for your own good, Dougie."

"Yeah, well, sometimes I'm so smart I get caught up in things I should leave well alone. Remember that caper in South Armagh?" He turned his head slightly to look over his shoulder at Pat and Gina. "If it hadn't been for Yvonne, Sergeant Mason as she was back then, I'd have been lucky to get out with just a couple of scratches."

"Just as well I was driving past." Yvonne winked at Dougie.

"Well, whatever. I owe you. Anyway, here we are. 'Woomera' is on pontoon C berth 10 — she's the white hulled cat over there." Dougie pointed it out. "She's fuelled up and water tanks are full. So, we're good to go as soon as you like."

The four of them climbed out of the vehicle, hoisted their bags over their shoulders and walked down the pier. As she climbed aboard, Yvonne looked around the catamaran.

"Very nice."

"Thanks. There are four cabins; two in each hull all en-suite and air-conditioned so we should be comfortable. The twin hulls give us stability and the wide platform at the back is great for diving. It's not quite as handy sailing up-wind but that wasn't the priority. I'm in the portside stern cabin by the way. Decide amongst yourselves which ones you're using."

After stowing their kit, they gathered in the cockpit with cans of beer.

"So, Yvonne, give. What's the game? And don't think I'm not coming with you. Life's been too quiet recently and I could do with a bit of adventure."

"It's your funeral," she said. "Can you get the chart of Bali?"

They spread the chart on the table and Yvonne started to outline the plan.

"ACE, that's our code name for the target, has a property in the south of Bali which includes a golf course. That's about 1000 nautical miles away. We'll island-hop from here to there taking around nine or ten days, stopping to dive at various points."

"OK. And when we get there?"

Yvonne outlined the plan.

"Beautiful," said Dougie.

"There are just a couple of things we're short of, Dougie. Can you lay your hands on some C4 and detonators?"

"I think I may have some left. You folks can check out the shipment and get stowed away while I go and get it. We'll head out for a bite to eat when I get back. Make sense?"

There was a general agreement.

The following morning, they cast off and motored out past the headland to the open water of the Timor Sea where the electric winches made easy work of hoisting the sails.

Woomera made her way westwards through the islands; hard driven passages under sail contrasting with days at anchor while the team dived the crystal-clear waters.

On the morning of the tenth day after leaving Darwin, they cruised round the southern tip of Penida Island, came head to wind while they dropped the sails and the anchor in around twenty metres of water off Manta Point.

Yvonne, Gina and Dougie put on their scuba kit and stepped off the platform at the stern of the boat — leaving Pat to manage Woomera; their turn would come later. Surfacing again, they gave each other the OK sign then deflated their BCDs and sank below the surface. They finned along the edge of the coral reef; streams of bubbles exhaled from their regulator mouthpieces heading to the surface.

Gina paused to take a photograph of a blue-green Napoleon wrasse and a school of parrotfish; adding to the evidence to show they were simply nature lovers. They were then rewarded with sight of the Manta Rays after which the location had been named. It would have been suspicious if they hadn't dived to see these impressive fish while in the area; and who knew how important it would be to have a water-tight alibi later?

From Manta Point, they sailed into the bay on the South-West coast of Bali — a couple of nautical miles up the coast from ACE's property. After anchoring, they all snorkelled off the boat before the sun set.

Under cover of darkness, Gina and Pat slipped into the water through the escape hatch under the saloon between the hulls. Yvonne then passed a small rubber dinghy to them which she then inflated and loaded with their equipment while they attached their underwater scooters either side of the inflatable's bow.

With less than twelve inches of freeboard, even if the inflatable was spotted from shore, it would probably be mistaken for a tree trunk drifting in the current. That was a very remote likelihood in any case as there was nothing offshore against which it could be silhouetted.

Gina and Pat towed the devices a couple of miles up the coast and anchored the inflatable eight hundred yards from the beach beyond an outcrop of coral. While Gina unpacked the kit and prepared the drone and bird for launch, Pat filled a net bag with rocks and hung it under the hull to provide stability. Their preparations complete, they switched their marine band radio to channel 20 and clicked the transmit button twice. They received an answering three clicks and watched as the drone controls were tested then signalled again with clicks on the radio.

Satisfied everything was ready, they put their masks back on and their mouthpieces in; checked how much air they had remaining, dropped below the surface once more and started back towards Woomera. Unhampered by towing the inflatable, they were soon under the catamaran's hull and climbing back on board.

The next morning, Dougie strapped on a tool belt, climbed into a bosun's chair and was hauled to the top of the mast where he appeared to be working on the wind indicator.

"OK, I think that's it," he called down.

In the cockpit, Gina switched on the drone controller. Two miles away, the drone rose out of the inflatable, lifting its payload to about three feet above the water. It skimmed the waves as it headed further away from Woomera before gradually climbing into the sky, blending in with the other dozen or so seabirds in the area. Back on the inflatable, small charges ignited, burning holes in the air chambers. As the air escaped, the remains sank below the surface dragged down by the weight of rocks suspended underneath until it settled on the bottom.

Yvonne operated the halyard winch to lower Dougie to the deck. Starting the twin diesels, she then raised the anchor, gently adjusting the throttles to keep the bow above the anchor line. Eventually, Dougie indicated that the anchor had been stowed and Yvonne turned Woomera into wind so they could hoist the main and unfurl the genoa. With the sails sheeted in, the catamaran left her mooring behind, the bows lifting and falling as she took the waves.

In the saloon, Gina's fingers played with the drone control. She could see from the laptop's GPS display that the bird, code name Eagle, suspended from the drone, code name Columbia, was just over four miles north of them at a height of six hundred feet. Next to her, Pat watched the display from Eagle's camera on a second laptop. The zoom lens showed the country club and golf course clearly — though they couldn't quite pick out individuals on the course.

Eagle and Columbia continued to climb as they approached the target area. At one mile out, they were at fifteen hundred feet and the players could easily be identified.

"Ready to release, Gina?" asked Pat.

"Ready."

"Go for it."

Gina pressed the switch to release the payload from Columbia. Eagle dipped down until Pat brought it back under control.

Released from its load, Columbia gained height as Gina turned it to head out to sea. Three miles offshore, she fired small charges to break the drone into pieces that scattered and sank on hitting the water.

Pat flew Eagle towards the group now driving down the fairway. Eagle circled silently overhead as ACE climbed out and walked to the bunker where his second shot had landed. As he took his sand wedge and adopted his stance by the ball, he became aware of a whistling above him. He looked up and saw Eagle swooping towards him.

As ACE's face filled the screen, Pat fired the claymore charge and fifty ball bearings spread out in a tight cone reaching just three feet diameter at ground level. Their calculations had been accurate and half a dozen stuck ACE.

"That's for Rita and Bobbi and the thousands of others whose lives you wasted," said Pat, wiping a tear from their cheek.

As Woomera rounded the southern tip of Bali, the crew dropped the two laptops and the drone controllers into more than three hundred feet of water.

About the author

Helen Dale Helen identifies as female with a transsexual history - her preferred pronouns are she/ her. She grew up as a RAF Brat and dreamed of being a pilot herself but failed the medical due to having had hay fever (the RAF considered it risky trying to land an aircraft and sneezing at the wrong moment).

Throughout her childhood and early career in PR, advertising and marketing and getting married and having a family, she concealed the secret that she was transgender.

In 1998, Helen accepted that she needed to transition. Losing one job as a consequence, Helen joined Greater Manchester Probation as IT Help Desk Manager in 1999. As the first openly trans employee nationally she provided awareness training for probation and prison staff (and others) and became the de facto lead on trans issues.

Helen persuaded the then Lesbian and Gay staff association (LAGIP) to extend its membership criteria to include trans and bisexual members and spent several years as chair. She also helped to found a:gender - the UK pan-Civil Service trans support network and was made an honorary life member when she retired in 2015.

She served on local and national diversity boards and chaired a trans charity in Manchester as well as training as a counsellor. Her work was recognised with several awards including a Butler Trust Award presented by HRH Princess Anne at Buckingham Palace.

Since retiring, Helen has continued to present workshops on trans issues and provide counselling for trans individuals. She also became a volunteer with Diversity Role Models - going into schools and talking to students about homophobic, transphobic and biphobic bullying.

Overall, Helen estimates that she's met well over 1,000 trans individuals who would previously been described as transsexual and many more who do not plan to transition permanently including cross-dressers, gender fluid, non-binary, drag artists/drag queens and some who identify as she-male. The discussions she's had with all of these individuals mean she has a huge wealth of information to draw on for her stories to ensure that they are authentic.

Helen started writing short stories for Cross Talk, Northern Concord Trans Support Group magazine, in the mid/ late 1990s — and started to write a novel while she was 'between contracts'. That novel was put on hold when she started working for Greater Manchester Probation in 1999.

After surgery in 2000, she joined Spice, a social activity group, in Manchester and did a number of adventurous events with them. This led to her colleagues asking, on Monday mornings, what she'd done at the weekend.

Typical answers were driving a tank, flying a jet, sailing a yacht, riding a quad bike or a hovercraft. Her colleagues told her that she'd led such an interesting life, she should write her autobiography — so she did.

While recollecting memories for it, she recalled an incident when she was 19 and living in London. She'd taken the train to Bournemouth, changing in the toilets at the end of the carriage and crossing over to Studland Bay and sunbathing in a bikini. She realised that she was being watched so left quickly.

But what if she hadn't noticed the guy?

What if he hadn't minded that she was trans?

That struck her as a possible start of a novel — which became 'Summer Dreams'.

Since retiring, Helen has been a member of the Manchester Women's Writers' Group which has provided valuable feedback on her work.

Check out Helen's website: www.helendaleauthor.info

Also by Helen Dale

Fiction

Summer Dreams

"Summer Dreams" is an authentic story of the transgender community and illustrates the wide range of trans people's experiences, the problems, prejudices and fears that they face (and some of their own prejudices) — and the fact that being trans is just one facet of their lives. It was inspired by a true incident when the author was about 19.

But let Vicky tell you about Summer Dreams:

I was David, but now I'm Vicky.

I was sunbathing in sand dunes near Bournemouth in 2003, when Roger found me and changed my life. After spending a heavenly holiday with him as Vicky, I just couldn't face reverting to David. I knew, though, that becoming Vicky permanently was impossible.

There was only one option, I tried to kill myself.

Roger saved me then showed how life as Vicky was possible.

Summer Dreams tells of my transition journey, coming out to family and friends and their reactions, some of which were very difficult to deal with, especially Peter my twin brother's and the abuse we faced from him and others.

But being trans is just part of who I am. Roger and I have a normal life too.

But is it too good to last?

Summer Dreams is an adult novel with explicit sex scenes

It is set in 2003-8 when the terms transvestite and transsexual were commonly used.

Impact

Chris's family don't know he cross-dresses.

If his wife ever found out, it could be the end of his marriage — and cost him his daughter.

But CAN his activities remain secret?

If not, what will the impact be?

Imposter

Jeff Shaw is transgender; he's been looking for a way of transitioning without causing financial problems for his family.

The train he's on is bombed and Michelle and Glen, two fellow passengers he's been talking to, are killed. Neither has family or friends to miss them and Jeff realises this is his opportunity for his male identity to be 'killed' in the incident and for him to reappear as Michelle.

But where did Michelle's substantial bank balance come from — and will it bring consequences in the future?

A Tale of Two Lives:

A Funny Thing Happened on the Way to the Palace

Inspirational story of award-winning trans activist, writer, trainer and counsellor: Helen Dale.

The story of growing up as a RAF Brat; concealing a secret for years; finally accepting what she was and doing something about it - and life after transition.

Having grown up as a RAF Brat and keen scout, dreaming of being a pilot in the RAF, I concealed a secret for decades before accepting, in 1998, that she needed to transition.

www.ingramcontent.com/pod-product-compliance
Lightning Source LLC
Chambersburg PA
CBHW061224210726
48294CB00006B/1969

9 781999 632953